The Natural World

BOOK HOUSE

Aberdeenshire

Published in Great Britain in MMXVII by
Book House, an imprint of
The Salariya Book Company Ltd
25 Marlborough Place, Brighton BN1 1UB
www.salariya.com

ISBN: 978-1-912006-74-8

SALARIYA

1 3 5 7 9 8 6 4 2

A CIP catalogue record for this book is available
from the British Library.

Printed and bound in China.
Printed on paper from sustainable sources.

Additional images from Shutterstock.

Visit
www.salariya.com
for our online catalogue and
fun **free** stuff.

ZAP!

The Natural World

Richard & Louise Spilsbury

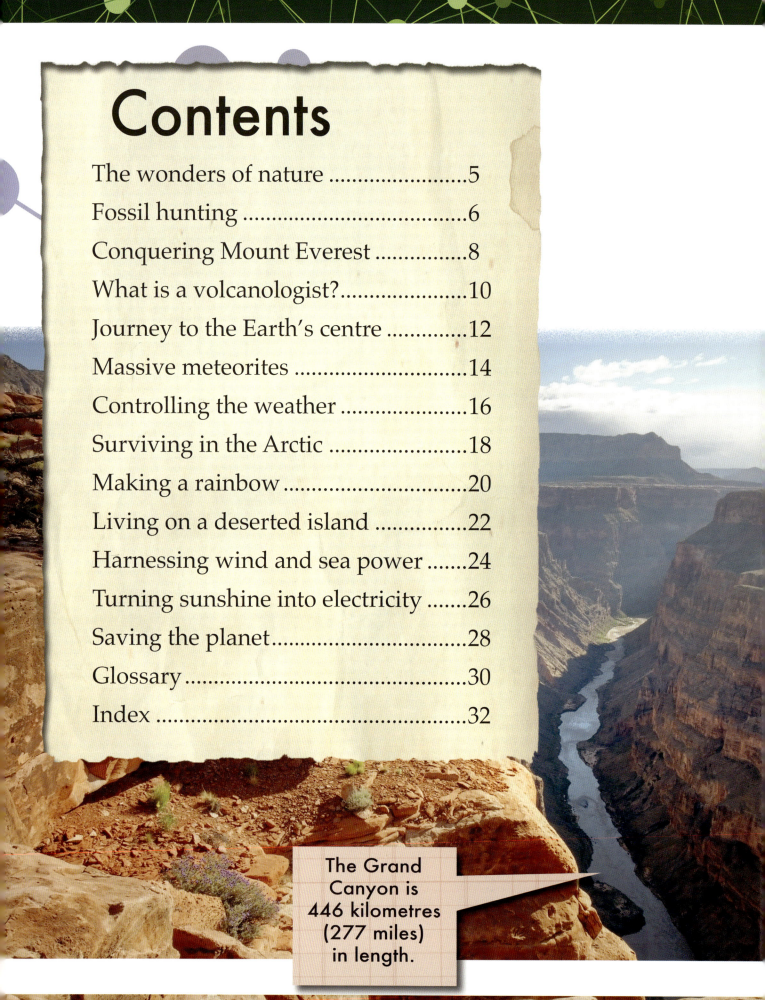

Contents

The Grand Canyon is 446 kilometres (277 miles) in length.

The wonders of nature

The natural world is full of wonders. There are mountains with peaks so high that they reach above the clouds, volcanoes that erupt and bring **molten** rock from inside the Earth to its surface, and rocks called fossils that hold the secrets to life on Earth.

Some of nature's wonders are small but still surprising – for example, the snowflake. No two snowflakes are ever the same, even though each one is formed when ice crystals join together in hexagonal (six-sided) shapes. Others wonders of nature are huge and awe-inspiring, such as the Grand Canyon in the United States. It took 10 million years for the Colorado River to wear away the land below to form this incredible, deep valley.

If you look closely, the faint outline of a hexagon at the centre of this snowflake can be seen.

Throughout this book we will look at many other wonders of nature and discover some amazing facts about how they came to be and what they are really like.

At its deepest point, the Grand Canyon is 1,829 metres (6,000 feet) high.

5

Fossil hunting

Today, we know a lot about dinosaurs because scientists have been able to piece together full-sized animals from fossils of their bones. Fossils are the remains of plants and animals that lived millions of years ago. These remains are usually preserved in rock. Most of the fossils people find are of ancient sea creatures, such as ammonites. Ammonites were giant sea snails.

Beaches at the base of cliffs are good places to find fossils but fossils can be found only in one type of rock: sedimentary rock.

Sedimentary rock is recognisable by its horizontal bands, or layers, of different colours.

People are still making amazing dinosaur discoveries today.

The rock cycle

All rocks on the Earth are constantly changing. Igneous rock forms from volcanic **magma**. Through **weathering** and **erosion**, igneous rock breaks down into **sediment**, which gradually forms into sedimentary rock. Under **pressure**, deep sedimentary rock can change into **metamorphic rock**.

The word fossil comes from the Latin word *fossilis*, which means 'dug up'.

How ammonite fossils form

1. A dead ammonite's soft body parts rot away.
2. The shell is buried in layers of sediment.
3. Water seeps into the shell and **minerals** from the water replace minerals in the shell.
4. The pressure of sediment above turns the minerals to rock, in the same shape as the original shell.

Mary Anning: fossil hunter

Mary Anning lived on the coast of Dorset in England. She was just 11 years old when she found the first **ichthyosaur** fossil skeleton. In the early 1800s, she also found a sea reptile, a plesiosaur (a prehistoric flying reptile), prehistoric fish and more. She hunted after storms, when cliffs crumbled to reveal new fossils.

The biggest ammonite ever found was 1.5 metres (5 ft) across.

The smallest dinosaur fossil is about the size of a chicken.

Conquering Mount Everest

At 8,848 metres (29,029 ft) tall, Mount Everest is the highest mountain in the world. Its height, freezing conditions and jagged peaks make it difficult to climb without a lot of effort, training, equipment and skill.

Climbing Mount Everest should be attempted in April and May, before the **monsoon** increases the risk of **avalanches**. Climbers could also try to reach the top in September after the monsoon and before winter storms bring the roaring winds, blinding snowstorms, thick clouds and icy cold temperatures that make climbing impossible.

The first people known to have reached the top of Everest are New Zealander Edmund Hillary and **Sherpa** Tenzing Norgay in 1953.

The area above 7,600 metres (24,934 ft) is known as the 'death zone' because of the harsh conditions and the risk of **altitude** sickness.

More than 280 people have died attempting to reach the top of Everest.

Altitude problems

The effects of high altitude on the human body are extreme. Higher up on a mountain, there is far less oxygen in the air because **gravity** holds it closer to the Earth's surface. If people climb too quickly, they can suffer from altitude sickness. This causes chest pain, breathing problems and can even kill.

Safety first

Climbers usually go with a Sherpa, a local guide who knows the best routes and can spot dangers. Teams also carry ropes to attach to rocks to keep climbers safe in exposed mountain locations. Oxygen tanks help them to breathe if they get altitude sickness.

Goggles protect eyes from snow blindness caused by the sun glaring off the snow.

Climbing kit

Layers of warm, waterproof clothing are vital for survival. It is freezing high up and winds make the temperature even colder. If melting ice and snow make climbers' feet or bodies damp, this increases the risk of **hypothermia**.

Crampons worn over boots have long spikes that grip ice.

Mount Everest grows about 4 millimetres (0.2 inches) a year.

9

What is a volcanologist?

Most volcanic eruptions are small but some are large and can cause terrible disasters. Volcanologists are scientists who study volcanoes and predict when they might erupt. They can help to keep people safe.

When a volcano erupts, it shoots out broken rocks and smoke with molten rock, called lava. As they fall, the rocks crush things and set them alight. A cloud of dust and ash makes the air black. The lava flows across the land and burns trees, buildings and anything else in its path.

How volcanologists help

- They use seismometer machines that detect earthquakes. Magma rising through cracks in the Earth's crust creates earthquakes.

- They use **thermal imaging** cameras and **satellites** that identify if a volcano is becoming hotter.

- They take gas samples from the volcano. The more sulphur in these gases, the closer the volcano is to erupting.

How volcanoes erupt

The Earth is a ball of molten metal, covered in a layer of cool, hard rock, called the crust. Sometimes, molten rock reaches the upper layer of the Earth's crust near a point of weakness. If pressure from the magma below builds up, it can erupt and burst through the surface.

There are more than 1,500 volcanoes on the Earth that could be active today.

A volcanic eruption

Volcanic islands

The cone shape of a volcano is made by layers of old lava from previous eruptions. When volcanoes cause eruptions on the sea floor, the lava that bursts out can poke above the water when it cools and hardens. This is how volcanic islands, such as Hawaii in the Pacific Ocean, are formed.

Deadly flows

A pyroclastic flow is a super-hot avalanche of ash and dust. It covers everything in a thick layer of ash. A lahar is a hot or cold mix of water and bits of rock that forms a kind of mud flow that can be fast and deadly, smothering any buildings in its way.

A volcanic island

The largest volcano is Mauna Loa in Hawaii, USA. Its lowest part is at the bottom of the sea.

Journey to the Earth's centre

Humans are always trying to go further out into space but they rarely attempt to venture deeper under the Earth's surface. One reason for this is the extreme heat that they would encounter as they travel towards the Earth's centre.

The Earth has four layers. The inner core is a ball of solid iron and **nickel** and it is the hottest part of the Earth. The outer core surrounding the inner core is a liquid layer, also made up of iron and nickel. The mantle is the widest section of the Earth. It consists of partly melted rock, called magma. The crust is the solid outer layer of rock that we live on.

The mantle is about 2,900 kilometres (1,800 miles) thick.

The crust is a thin layer between 0 and 60 kilometres (37 miles) thick.

The inner core has temperatures of up to 5,500 degrees Celsius (9,932 degrees Fahrenheit).

The outer core has temperatures similar to the inner core.

The upper mantle is hard rock but lower down, the rock is soft and molten.

Under pressure

As well as the heat, another challenge beneath the Earth's surface is the pressure caused by the mass of rock above. The deeper people go, the greater the pressure. At 1,000 metres (3,281 ft) deep, the pressure is the same as having four elephants balanced on a person's head.

Deepest caves

The most common caves form when rainwater soaks underground. Minerals dissolved in the water wear away soft limestone rock to create cracks and caves. At 2,197 metres (7,208 ft) deep, Krubera Cave in Georgia is the deepest cave in the world.

Drilling deep

Boreholes are deep, narrow holes drilled into the Earth. They can be used to collect resources or to investigate what is there. Sometimes, boreholes are drilled down into aquifers (rocks that store water that has soaked underground). A pump is used to extract the water and bring it to the surface.

Mining challenges

Working in underground mines can be hot and dangerous work. At 3,900 metres (12,795 ft) deep in the TauTona gold mine in South Africa, rock faces can reach temperatures of around 60°C (140°F).

Explorers have travelled 2 kilometres (1.2 miles) down into Krubera Cave.

13

Massive meteorites

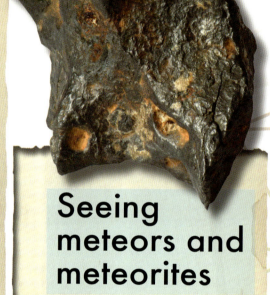

Meteorites are bits of space rock that have fallen to Earth. Most meteorites that crash on Earth are small. Some are huge. A meteorite created Barringer Crater, in Arizona, United States. Barringer Crater is a huge pit that is 1,200 metres (4,000 ft) in diameter and about 180 metres (600 ft) deep.

When bits of rock **orbit** in space, they are called meteoroids. If meteoroids stray into a planet's **atmosphere**, they burn up. Then, they are known as meteors. If a space rock survives its trip through our planet's atmosphere and reaches the Earth's surface, then it is called a meteorite.

Shooting stars

Shooting stars are really meteors burning up in the Earth's atmosphere. Some meteors are bits of dust and rock that are left behind from a comet's tail. When the Earth's orbit takes it through thick comet debris, meteor showers happen. This is when many meteors are seen in one night.

Seeing meteors and meteorites

The best chance of seeing meteors is during a meteor shower. Meteor showers light up the sky several times a year. To maximise the number of meteors seen, people should head away from city lights and pollution to somewhere with a clear, unclouded view of the night sky. Meteorites are easiest to find on polar ice or desert sand when there are no other rocks around.

Most meteorites are bits of **asteroids** but some are from the moon and Mars.

Clues to the past

Meteorites can give clues about how the Earth's solar system evolved into the sun and planets of today. Some meteorites contain the first solid material to form in the Earth's solar system. Researchers have used the age of this material – 4.568 billion years – to work out the age of the Earth's solar system.

Statistics

- Some scientists believe that a massive meteorite crash may have caused thick clouds of dust that blocked the sun's rays and caused the extinction of the dinosaurs.
- Every day, about 50 tonnes of rocky material from space lands on the Earth's surface.
- Meteoroids range in size from grains of dust to the size of a house.

Barringer Crater is about 50,000 years old.

Barringer Crater is also known as Meteor Crater.

The dry desert has preserved the crater well.

Over 70 percent of the Earth is covered in water so most meteorites fall into the oceans.

Controlling the weather

Rain can be a nuisance when it stops a picnic or prevents farmers from harvesting crops, but we do need it. Without rain to water plants and fill **reservoirs**, crops would not grow and people would not have enough water to drink or to wash and cook with.

Even in dry places in the world, there is always moisture in the sky in the form of a gas called water vapour. People are trying out new methods of forcing clouds to release their water as rain during times of **drought**.

Rain shadows

Mountains can make it rain. When winds blow clouds towards mountains, the clouds are forced to rise up the slopes. As they rise, they become colder and the water in them condenses and falls as rain. The moisture in the clouds gets used up so the area beyond a mountain gets hardly any rain and becomes very dry.

The area beyond a mountain can become a desert because of the rain shadow effect.

How rain forms

The sun's heat warms water on the Earth's surface, causing it to **evaporate** and turn from a liquid into water vapour. As the water vapour rises and cools, it **condenses** and turns from a gas into a liquid. If these water droplets condense on dust, salt or smoke **particles**, they form droplets of water that fall as rain.

The process in which water constantly moves between the atmosphere and the Earth's surface is called the water cycle.

Cloud seeding

Scientists try to make rain fall by a process called cloud seeding. In cloud seeding, aeroplanes fly into clouds and release packets of **microscopic** particles of **chemicals**. Water droplets can form around these particles. After 20 or 30 minutes, the water droplets should be big and heavy enough to fall as rain.

Monsoons

From May each year, monsoon winds bring heavy rain and storms to countries in south and southeast Asia. The rains happen when warm air rises over the hot land in summer, and is replaced by cool, very moist air from the ocean. This moist air releases its water as heavy rains.

The monsoon rains can cause floods.

During a monsoon season, there are also thousands of lightning strikes.

Surviving in the Arctic

The Arctic, or North Pole, is a huge, frozen ocean and one of the coldest places on the planet. In summer, the far edges of the ocean melt, but in winter, the whole area is completely frozen over. In winter at the Poles, there is 24 hours of darkness and temperatures drop drastically.

Life in the Arctic is harsh and challenging. Icy winds can freeze bare skin in seconds, snowstorms can make it hard to see and it is very easy to become lost. People move around on land using snowmobiles. When they travel by sea in the Arctic, they need to watch out for floating **icebergs**.

Keeping warm

If people get too cold, they can suffer from hypothermia and die. To keep warm, they should wear layers of clothes or animal skins. They should also keep their fingers, nose and other **extremities** covered. They also need a shelter. An igloo is a type of shelter used in the Arctic. It is a circle of ice blocks that curve in to meet at a dome-shaped roof when piled up.

Food and water

It is very dry at the North Pole so the people who visit there can easily become thirsty. They should never melt snow in their mouths because this will make them even colder. Instead, they should make a fire from dried moss and animal droppings and use this to melt ice or snow in a pan. In the Arctic, it is too cold for plants to grow so people need to catch and eat fish or the seabirds and seals that eat the fish.

The ice of the Arctic contains around 10 percent of the world's fresh water.

The South Pole

Antarctica, or the South Pole, is just as cold and challenging as the Arctic. Antarctica is the Earth's fifth-largest **continent**. It is covered with a sheet of ice that is more than 3 kilometres (1.9 miles) thick. In winter, the surface of the ocean around it freezes over. Temperatures at the South Pole can drop to below -73°C (-100°F) in winter.

Polar bears

Polar bears are found only at the North Pole. They do not normally attack people, but a hungry polar bear might do so to feed itself and its hungry cubs. A polar bear can run faster than a person on land and it can kill **prey** with just one swipe of its mighty paws.

Snowmobiles are motorised sledges with rubber tracks and rough treads that grip the ground and do not sink in the snow.

Making a **rainbow**

Rainbows are such an amazing sight that people used to think that there was something magical about them. In a way, there is, because rainbows do not really exist. They are an optical illusion – a trick of the light.

Sunlight looks white but it is actually made up of different colours that people do not usually see. If the light rays that beam towards the Earth hit raindrops at a certain angle, the different colours that make up white light separate so that we can see them in a beautiful rainbow.

Refract and reflect

When a ray of white light shines into a raindrop, the ray refracts (bends) and **reflects** off the back of the raindrop. This is what separates the colours within white light and makes them visible. These different colours then spread out to form a rainbow.

Speed of light

The colours inside white light slow down at different speeds when they enter a raindrop. This means that people see only one colour coming from each raindrop, depending on the angle the light travelled in. Light at different angles coming through many raindrops forms the rainbow of colours.

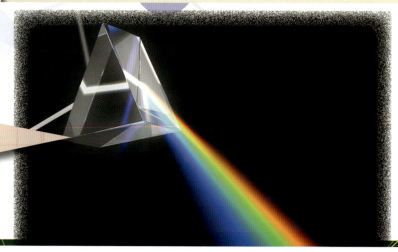

A prism is a wedge-shaped glass object that can split white sunlight into its different colours.

A rainbow is a circle of light but only a semi-circle is visible because people view it from the ground.

There are seven colours in a rainbow: red, orange, yellow, green, blue, indigo and violet.

Seeing rainbows

We usually see rainbows after a rain shower. They can also be seen when fog or misty clouds create moisture in the air, or in the spray in a waterfall. People can even make a rainbow by flashing a CD in sunshine.

People see a whole rainbow because they are looking at many raindrops, all bending and separating the sun's light.

You can make a rainbow by standing with your back to the sun and spraying a fine mist with a garden hose.

Mirages

Mirages happen when light is refracted. In a mirage, people think that they see water over a desert or hot road. In fact, when light rays from a blue sky pass through cool into warm air, they are refracted upwards. The brain sees blue light coming from the ground and thinks it is water.

Light from the moon can produce a rare night-time rainbow called a 'moonbow'.

Living on a deserted island

If an aeroplane crash-lands or a boat sinks in the sea, the survivors may end up on a deserted island. It is not as hard as one might think to survive on a desert island. Some people end up living on them for a long time.

Survivors need to be aware of wild animals. They also need to watch where they step because some snakes and insects bite. To keep away from poisonous snakes that slither on the ground, people should make a hammock or a raised platform to sleep on.

Safe from the sun

Shelters are useful for protecting people from the sun's harsh rays. When sunlight reflects off the sea and light-coloured sand, it can burn the skin and cause heat stroke. Heat stroke stops the body being able to cool down. When the body overheats, this causes brain damage, and in extreme cases, death.

Drinking water

Some islands have freshwater streams that survivors can drink from. They can also drink the watery milk inside coconuts. With a bit of effort, salt water can be converted to drinking water. To do this, the water must be boiled until it turns to steam. The steam must then be captured. When this steam condenses, it becomes safe water to drink because the water evaporates but the salt does not.

A deserted island is an island with no people on it.

Building a shelter

A lot of water evaporates from the sea during the day and falls again as rain overnight, so survivors need a roof over their heads to stay as dry as possible.

Shelters can be built from cloth, boat sails or pieces of wood washed up on the shore. The roof can be made from branches and leaves.

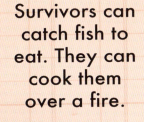

Survivors can catch fish to eat. They can cook them over a fire.

Smoke signals

To escape the island, those who are stranded need to signal for help. During the day, they can flash a mirror by reflecting sunlight off it to send signals to boats and aircraft. At night, they can signal with a torch or build three fires in a row. A line of three fires is an international signal that tells others someone needs help.

Look out for sea snakes – they are usually extremely poisonous.

Harnessing wind and sea power

There is a lot of energy in the wind and the waves on the ocean that are whipped up by the **tides**. This energy can be harnessed and used to make electricity.

One advantage of energy from different types of weather is that, unlike **fossil fuels**, they will not run out. They are called renewable energy sources. Fossil fuels, such as oil, coal and gas, take millions of years to form so when they run out, there will be no more of them. They are non-renewable.

How fossil fuels form

Fossil fuels are so-named because they formed from the remains of plants and animals that died millions of years ago. After the plants and animals died and became buried in sediment, the heavy weight of the rock forming above their remains helped to turn them into fuels.

Wind power

Wind **turbines** are tall towers with metal blades at the top. Wind pushing against the blades makes them turn and **generators** convert this movement energy into a flow of electricity. The towers hold the blades up high, where wind speeds are faster than they are at ground level.

Wind turbine blades can spin at 290 kilometres per hour (180 miles per hour).

Wave power

The movement of the tides can be turned into electricity, too. The turbines that form a tidal power station are connected to a generator, which converts the movement of the tides into electrical energy. The turbines look very similar to wind turbines but they are specially designed to work under water.

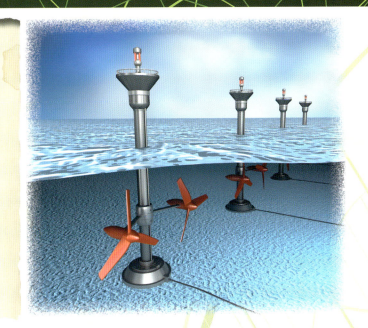

Wind farms are groups of turbines that are built near each other in windy places.

Problems with sea and wind power

- Tidal power stations can generate electricity for only about ten hours each day, when the tide is flowing in or out.
- Tidal power stations must be able to withstand rough weather and waves.
- Wind turbines can be noisy and the blades can kill birds.
- Some people dislike the appearance of the wind turbines in the countryside.
- Wind turbines work only when the wind is blowing.

Denmark generates nearly 20 percent of its electricity from wind.

Turning sunshine into electricity

The sun is a powerful source of energy. Its heat and light are so strong that they can still burn people after travelling millions of miles through space and the Earth's atmosphere. People have been harnessing the sun's energy to make electricity for a long time.

The advantages of solar power are that it is renewable, it can be used in remote places that do not have access to the main **power grid**, and it causes much less pollution than burning fossil fuels to make electricity.

Solar thermal power

Solar thermal power stations have banks of mirrors that focus sunlight onto a small area. The mirrors tilt to follow the sun. This energy is used to heat a liquid to an extremely hot temperature. The hot liquid produces steam that drives a turbine connected to a generator to make electricity.

Solar panels do not generate electricity. Instead, they heat up water to do this.

Panels are often placed on the roofs of buildings where they can receive heat energy from the sun.

Sunlight is by far the largest source of energy received by the Earth.

Photovoltaic cells

Photovoltaic systems produce electricity directly from sunlight. Photovoltaic cells are thin discs of **silicon** sandwiched together. When sunlight hits the cells, electrons inside the cells are released. These produce an electric current that can be used as electricity.

Statistics

- The energy absorbed by the ocean, land and air from the sun in just 1.5 hours could power the Earth for a whole year.
- The world's energy could be supplied by covering less than 1 percent of the Earth's surface with solar panels.

Biomass plant

Plants use energy from sunlight to grow, and these natural materials store sunlight in the form of chemical energy. Biomass is natural material, such as wood, wood waste, straw, manure and sugar cane, which is burnt to release that energy to make heat that powers turbines and generators.

A solar thermal plant in Morocco covers the same area as the country's capital – Rabat.

Saving the planet

The Earth's wonderful natural world is under threat. In the past, natural causes created problems – for example, meteorites may have caused the mass **extinction** of the dinosaurs 65 million years ago. Today, humans are responsible for many of the risks facing the environment.

When people clear forests and other **habitats** to make space for mines, buildings and other things, animals lose their homes. The waste that people produce and the fuels that they burn pollute the air, land and water. The burning of fuels also contributes to another huge problem: global warming.

Global warming

When fossil fuels are burnt to generate energy, this releases gases into the atmosphere that contribute to global warming. These gases help to trap heat near the Earth's surface and are causing the Earth's temperature to increase.

Melting ice will increase sea levels.

Recycling aluminium reduces greenhouse gas emissions.

Problems with global warming

As a result of global warming there may be more natural disasters in the future. As the Earth gets hotter, there will be more hurricanes, fires and droughts. When ice at the poles melts, the level of the sea will rise, causing more floods.

Reuse and recycle

If people reduce waste and buy and use less, they reduce the amount of habitats disrupted by mines and buildings. The amount of fuel burnt to make and deliver goods is also reduced, and so is the water that is used or polluted by factories and farms.

Global warming is endangering some animals including the Adélie penguin.

What can be done

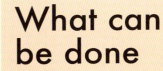

Do not use any more packaging than is necessary.

- Use reusable bags rather than plastic carrier bags when shopping.
- Recycle as much as possible, including bottles, cans, papers and clothes.
- Make a **compost** heap to recycle food waste such as vegetable peelings.

Global warming could make deserts bigger and cause food shortages in many places.

Glossary

Altitude Height above sea level or ground level.

Asteroids Small, rocky bodies orbiting the sun that are larger than meteors but smaller than planets.

Atmosphere The blanket of gases surrounding a planet.

Avalanches Large amount of snow and ice or rocks that moves and slides suddenly down the side of a mountain.

Chemicals Anything made of matter – any solid, liquid or gas.

Compost Decayed food and garden waste used as a fertiliser for growing plants.

Condenses The process of a gas turning into a liquid when it cools and contracts.

Continent A large landmass.

Drought Little or no rain.

Erosion When wind, rain, ice or moving water move away bits of rock that have been weathered on a rock surface.

Evaporate To change from a liquid into a gas. When liquid water warms up it can evaporate and turn into water vapour, a gas in the air.

Extinction To completely die out.

Extremities Outermost parts of the body, such as the fingers and nose.

Fog A thick cloud of tiny water droplets floating in the air near the Earth's surface.

Fossil fuels Coal, oil or gas that formed from the remains of plants and animals that died millions of years ago.

Generators Machines that make electricity.

Gravity A natural force that causes objects to move towards each other.

Habitats Places where plants and animals usually live.

Hypothermia A condition in which the body gets too cold to function properly.

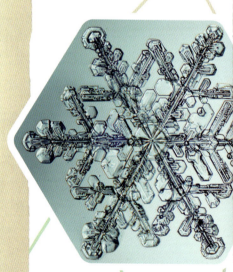

Icebergs Large floating masses of ice.

Ichthyosaur Fossil of an ancient animal that was like a dolphin.

Magma Hot, liquid rock found below the surface of the Earth.

Metamorphic rock Rock created by the transformation of other types of rock.

Microscopic Describes something so small it can be seen only with the help of a microscope.

Minerals Substances such as coal, oil or gold that are naturally formed under the ground.

Molten Melted.

Monsoon Winds that bring heavy rains to parts of South and Southeast Asia, from May to September each year.

Nickel A silvery-white metal.

Orbit A curved path around an object in space.

Particles Very, very tiny pieces of a substance.

Power grid A network of electricity stations and power lines.

Pressure A pushing force.

Prey An animal that is caught and eaten by other animals.

Reflects Bounces back.

Reservoirs Lakes made by people to collect and store water.

Satellites Machines placed in orbit round the Earth or another planet in order to collect information or for communication.

Sediment Materials such as sand, soil and stones that can sink to the bottom of a liquid.

Sherpa A member of a Himalayan group of people living on the borders of Nepal and Tibet.

Silicon A material that can be used to make electrical circuits.

Thermal imaging Making pictures of things using the heat that they give off.

Tides The movement of the sea up and down a shore.

Turbines Machines with blades that rotate and capture energy.

Weathering The wearing away of the surface of rocks by wind, heat, cold, rain and moving water.

Index